THE EVENT

DANIEL GRANT

PART 5

ISBN-13: 978-1-948297-20-2

DALLENT

AND -- WHY IN THE WORLD AREN'T YOU WEARING YOUR USUAL REGALIA.

NOT THAT IT REALLY MATTERS HOW ONE DRESSES FOR THEIR BEHEADING.

THEY DO SOME REALLY ELABORATE ROLE PLAYING AROUND HERE.

I'M JUST A BIT INCOGNITO TODAY. I'D REALLY LIKE TO KEEP IT THAT WAY.

TELL ME ABOUT IT.

BEFORE YOU TAKE MY HEAD, YOU MIGHT WANT TO HEAR WHAT I HAVE TO SAY.

I MIGHT HAVE A SOLUTION TO OUR MUTUAL MOST PRESSING PROBLEM.

INTERESTING!

I THINK SO!

THERE ARE MANY *HORNY SLUTS* IN THE *WORLD,* OBANNION.

SHE *ALSO NEEDS* TRAINING *BEFORE* WE GIVE HER *ACCESS* TO THE *SCROLL* AND THE *HOLY OF HOLIES.*

ASSUMING SHE CAN EVEN *MANAGE* TO *PASS THROUGH* THE *GATEWAY?*

I THINK A *FURTHER TEST* IS *REQUIRED* BEFORE I *THROW* MY SUPPORT BEHIND *YOURS.*

WHAT *MANNER* OF TEST?

THE *PROPHECY* SAYS *SCHERAZADE* WILL *NAVIGATE* THE *DOMAINS INNATELY.*

AND -- *READILY* OPEN THE *DOORS* BETWEEN THEM.

WELL, THE *PROPHECY* SAYS A *LOT* OF THINGS.

A **HH HH**

WE CAN'T *PICK* AND *CHOOSE* O'BANNION.

I *SUPPOSE* YOU'RE *RIGHT*, BUT IF WE *DELAY* IN *ORDER* TO EFFECTIVELY *TRAIN* HER, SOME OF US MIGHT *NOT* MAKE IT.

OHH

FAIRCHILD IS *PARTICULARLY* VULNERABLE.

IF WE *DON'T*, WHO *KNOWS* WHAT SHE *IS* OR MIGHT *DO*.

SO NOW YOU' *SUSPECT* SHE'S A *GUILD SPY*, CHEN?

YOU *KNOW* THAT'S *JUST* RIDICULOUS.

DOES SHE *LOOK LIKE* THE *TYPICAL* COLLEGE PROFESSOR TO *YOU*, MOLLY?

THE WHOLE *POINT* OF THE *TRAINING* IS TO *INSURE* ONLY *TRUE BELIEVERS* ARE GIVEN *ACCESS* TO THE *TRUTH*.

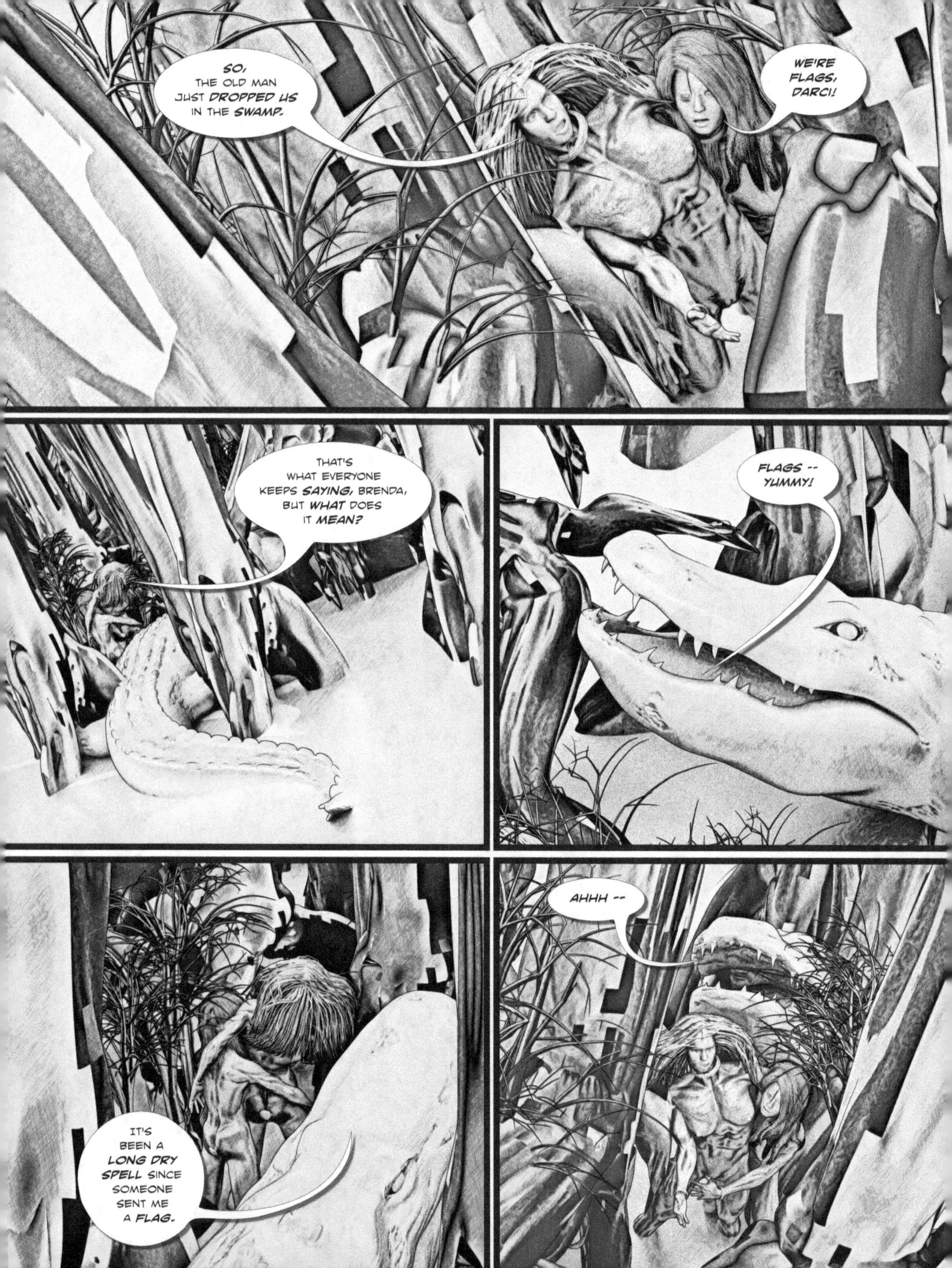

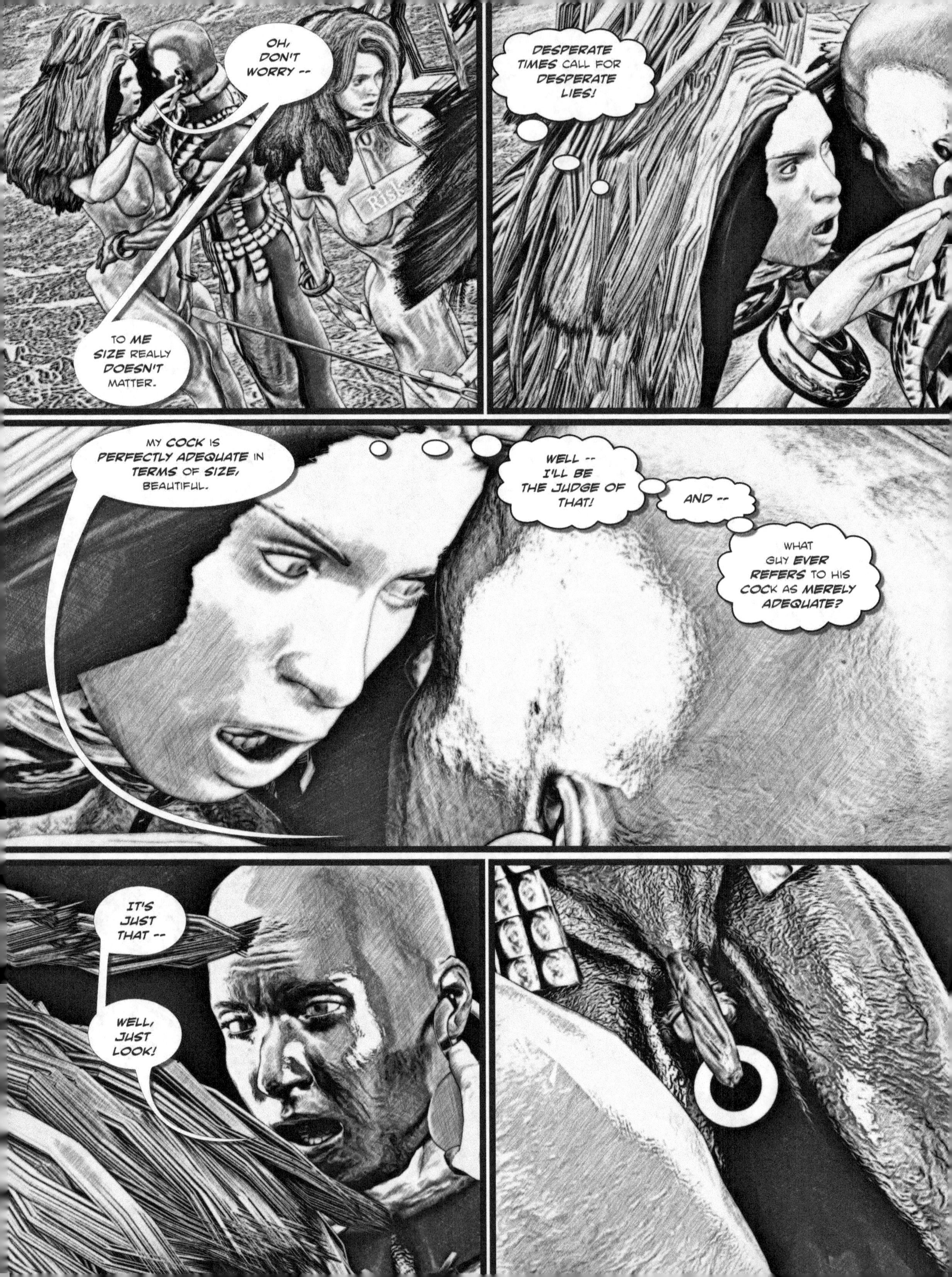

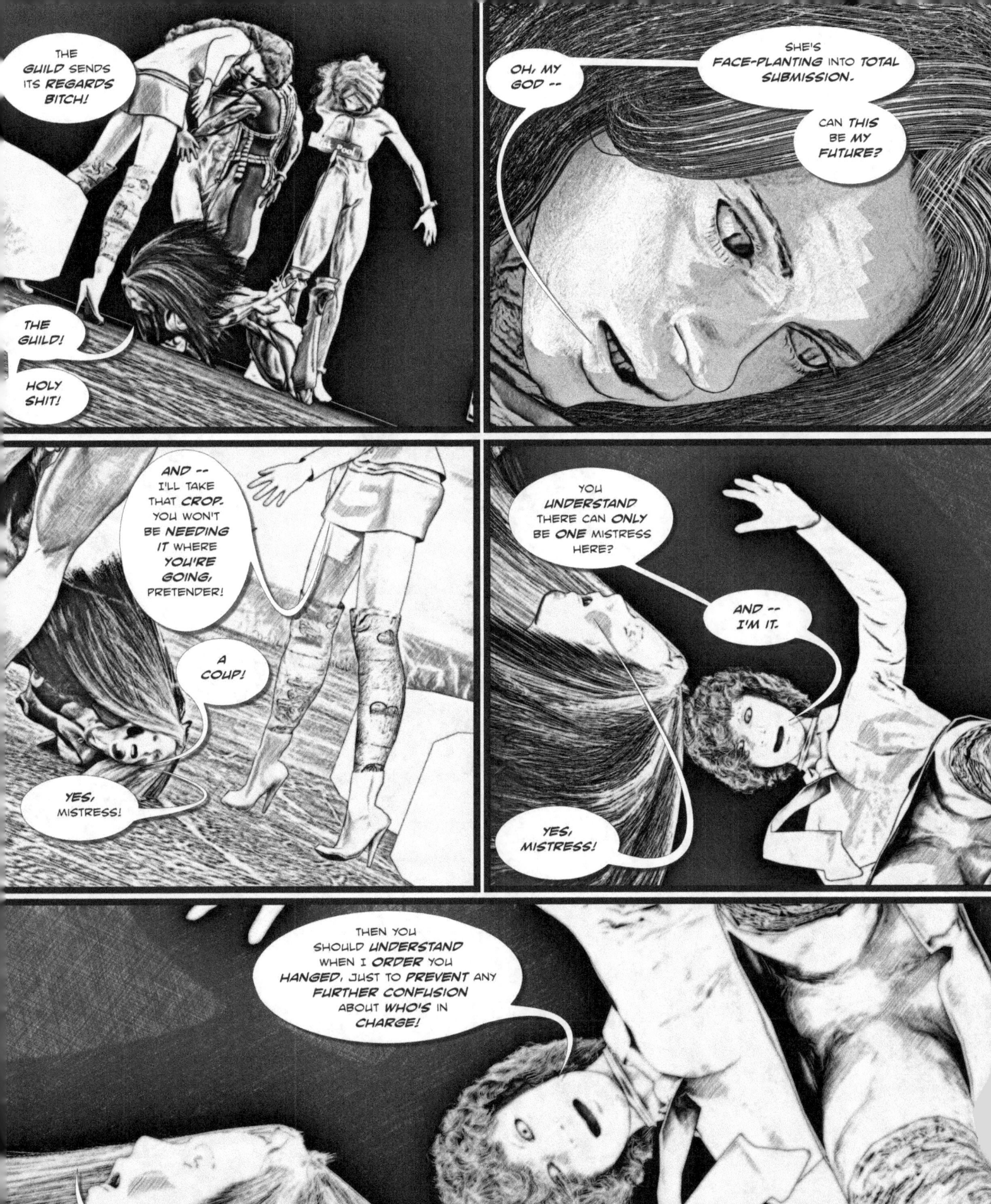